Teeny Weeny Bop

Margaret Read MacDonald   Illustrated by Diane Greenseid

Albert Whitman & Company, Morton Grove, Illinois

For the bookophiles who keep me bopping along:
George Shannon, Meg Lippert, Sally Porter, and Mie Mie Wu. And of
course for Cordelia Squealia, the newest teller in my family.—M.R.M.

For Beth, Mark, and Marsha, my big boppin' teeny-weeny crew with lots of heart.—D.G.

Library of Congress Cataloging-in-Publication Data

MacDonald, Margaret Read, 1940-
Teeny Weeny Bop / by Margaret Read MacDonald ; illustrated by Diane Greenseid.
p. cm.
Summary: Upon finding a gold coin, a lonely woman trades it for a pig,
then a succession of smaller, less troublesome pets.
ISBN-13: 978-0-8075-7992-3 (hardcover)
ISBN-10: 0-8075-7992-0 (hardcover)
[1. Folklore—Great Britain.] I. Greenseid, Diane, ill. II. Title.
PZ8.1.M15924Tee 2006 398.20941'02—dc22 2005024623

The design is by Diane Greenseid and Carol Gildar.

For more information about Albert Whitman & Company, visit our web site at www.albertwhitman.com.

One morning Teeny Weeny Bop was sweeping her floor.
She was sweeping her floor and sweeping her floor and . . .
she found a gold coin in a crack in her floor!

"My luck is MADE! I'll go to town and buy myself a little pet pig.
I won't have to live alone anymore."

Off she went down the road . . . just a-singing!

To market, to market! To buy a fat PIG!
Home again, home again! Jiggety-JIG!

"Mr. Pet Man, I want to trade my gold coin for a little pet pig."

"Gold coin for a pig? Good enough trade. Pick out any pig you want."

"I'll take that fat little pig right . . . *there!*"

I went to market and I bought a fat PIG!
Going back home again. Jiggety-JIG!

"Now, where can I keep my pig?" she wondered.

"I know—I'll put him in the garden. He'll be safe in there."

She went to bed, she went to sleep, she snored, snored, snored!
What do you think that pig did during the night?

"OH, NO!"
He rooted up her carrots.
He rooted up potatoes.
He rooted up her turnips.
Rooted up her rutabagas!

PIG! PIG! What a MESS you've MADE!
I'm taking you to market
and I'm going to TRADE!

"I'll trade for a better pet. I'll get myself
a . . . CAT!"

To market, to market! To buy a fat CAT!
Home again, home again! Jiggety-JAT!

"Mr. Pet Man, can I trade my pig for a cat?"

"A pig for a cat? Good enough trade. Take any cat you want."

"I'll take that fat white one right . . . *there.*"

*I went to market and I bought a fat CAT!
Going back home again. Jiggety-JAT!*

"But where can I keep my cat?"

"I'll keep him in the living room. He'll be safe in here."

She went to bed, she went to sleep, she snored, snored, snored!
What do you think that cat did during the night?

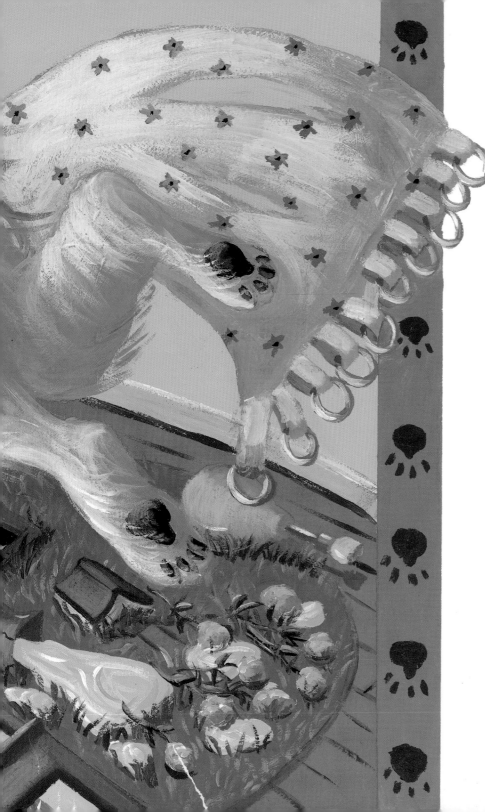

"OH, NO!"
He scratched the sofa.
He clawed the drapes.
He ripped the carpet.
He broke the vase!

CAT! CAT! What a MESS you've MADE!
I'm taking you to market
and I'm going to TRADE!

"I'll get myself a . . . HAMSTER!"

To market, to market!
To buy a fat HAMSTER!
Home again, home again!
Jiggety-JAMSTER!

"Mr. Pet Man, can I trade my cat for a hamster?"
"Cat for a hamster? Good enough trade. Pick out any one you want."
"I'll take that fat little one right . . . *there!*"

I went to market and I bought a fat HAMSTER!
Going back home again. Jiggety-JAMSTER!

"But where can I keep my hamster?"

"I'll keep him in the . . . kitchen cupboard! He'll be safe in there!"
She went to bed, she went to sleep, she snored, snored, snored!
What do you think that hamster did during the night?

"OH, NO!"
He ate up all the crackers.
He crunched the cornflakes.
He gnawed into the cookies.
He chawed into the cake!

HAMSTER! HAMSTER!
What a MESS you've MADE!
I'm taking you to market
and I'm going to TRADE!

"Let me see . . . I want something smaller.
I want a pet with no teeth . . . and no claws . . .
I know! A SLUG! A SLUG can't do any harm!"

To market, to market!
To buy a fat SLUG!
Home again, home again!
GLUGGETY-GLUG!

"Mr. Pet Man, can I trade my hamster for a pet slug?"

"Hamster for a slug? Good enough trade. Pick out any slug you want, ma'am."

"I want that really fat one right . . . there!"

I went to market and I bought a fat SLUG!
Going back home again. GLUGGETY-GLUG!

"Now where can I keep my slug?"

"He likes it cool . . . and damp . . .
I'll keep him in the refrigerator!
He'll be safe in there."

She went to bed, she went to sleep, she dreamed a silly dream.
What do you think that slug did during the night?

"OH, NO!"
He slimed the cabbage.
He slimed the cheese.
He slimed the jello.
He slimed the peas!

SLUG! SLUG! What a MESS you've MADE!
I'm taking you to market and I'm going to TRADE!

"These pets are just NOT working out.
I'm going to trade for my gold coin back."

To market, to market! To get my gold coin!
To market, to market! Gonna get my gold coin!

"Mr. Pet Man. I want to trade this slug for my gold coin."
"Gold coin for a *slug?* NO, MA'AM. That's a bad trade."
"Oh. Well, then I'll trade this slug for my PIG."
"Pig for a *slug?* NO, MA'AM. That's a bad trade."
"Well, then give me my CAT back."

"Cat for a *slug?* NO, MA'AM."

"Could I have my HAMSTER back then?"

"Hamster for a *slug?* NO, MA'AM."

"Well, this doesn't seem right. I had a gold coin a while ago. Then I had a PIG . . . then I had a CAT . . . then I had a HAMSTER . . .

"Now all I've got left is a SLUG? I don't even want it! You can have it back!"

I went to market but I couldn't even trade.
I went to market but . . .

I couldn't . . .

even . . .

trade.

Teeny Weeny Bop went home and started sweeping her floor.
She was sweeping her floor and sweeping her floor and . . .
she found a SILVER coin in a crack in her floor!

"MY LUCK IS MADE! I'll buy myself another pet! Think I'll buy

To market, to market! To buy a fat HOG!
Home again, home again! Jiggety-JOG!

No more, no more, Teeny Weeny Bop!
Your silly story has got to . . . STOP!

Note

This story is put together from several folktale motifs. The idea of a woman racing off to buy a pet after finding a coin appears in several folktales in the British tradition. Katherine Briggs's *British Folk-Tales* (Bloomington, Indiana: Indiana University Press, 1970) mentions seven such tales. And stories about foolish folks who repeatedly make bad bargains are popular worldwide. (Folklorists call this: *Motif J2081.1 Foolish bargain: horse for cow, cow for hog, etc., finally nothing left.*) To give a bounce to my story, I added a refrain based on the old nursery rhyme chant, "To market, to market!" I was inspired to write this story after reading a different folktale about a teeny weeny bop in a collection by an Australian educator, Jean Chapman (*Tell Me Another Tale*, Nottinghamshire, England: Award Publications Limited, 1976).